LOOKING
to the
CLOUDS
for
DADDY

Written by Margo Candelario

Illustrated by Jerry Craft

Published by Karen Hunter Media
1180 Raymond Blvd. - Suite 7J
Newark, NJ 07102

This book is dedicated to my husband Phil
who will always be remembered
everytime I look at my three girls,
past and present.
- Margo Candelario

KAREN HUNTER MEDIA

Karen Hunter Media
1180 Raymond Blvd.- Suite 7J
Newark, NJ 07102

Karen Hunter Media is a trademark of Karen Hunter Media, LLC.
All rights reserved, including the right of reproduction in whole or in part or in any form.

Looking to the Clouds for Daddy / Written by Margo Candelario / Illustrated by Jerry Craft
Text copyright © 2009 by Margo Candelario / Illustration copyright © 2009 by Jerry Craft
Designed by Jerry Craft

Manufactured in Mexico

ISBN-13: 978-0-9820221-7-7
ISBN-10: 0-9820221-7-4

First Edition
Printed in Mexico

To order additional copies of this book call
Karen Hunter Publishing at
800.513.9368
or visit the website at
www.readourbooks.com

See Margo Candelario's
poetry, writing and paintings at
www.margocandelario.com

Jerry Craft's Mama's Boyz comic strip,
illustrations and Flash animation
www.mamasboyz.com

FOREWORD

I first met Margo when she and the girls moved to our school district and Cheyenne began attending our elementary school. Margo immediately struck me as energetic, creative, positive, and resourceful. Her hearty and sincere laughter immediately drew me to her, and our mutual love of the arts built on that friendship.

Cheyenne, Camaryn and Trae have all graduated from our school, but during their years with us I found myself watching with admiration the ways in which Margo was able to be a loving and supportive parent, as well as one of the most innovative women I know. In what I consider to be a short amount of time, Margo has built a strong international recognition for her art, poetry and writing. Yet, at the same time, she has taught her girls to strive, thrive and survive!

Margo and her daughters have flourished in a world that presents many challenges to struggling artists and single parents. I think she would agree that those challenges, and the knowledge that Phil has always been an underlying support for her talent and ideas, have made her, Cheyenne, Camaryn and Trae strong, versatile, successful, and accomplished women!

Congratulations, Margo! This book is a gift to the many children who struggle with the loss of a parent and who search for comfort and understanding.

Marilyn Wolf-Ragatz, EDD

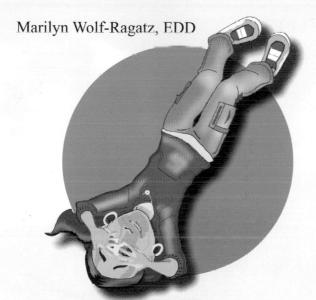

My name is Cheyenne. And on bright, sunny days, when the color of the sky looks like a blue popsicle with cotton balls stuck on it...

...my sisters and I hunt for our favorite spot in the yard.
A place for daydreaming
and good memories.

With no big trees or tall grass to block the view,
we lay down on our backs, peeking and squinting
through eyelashes and fingers,
studying the clouds.

There are giant
cumulus clouds
that look like big
floating pillows.
And stratus clouds
that Camaryn and
Trae have nicknamed
"stringus,"
because they are
stretchy and stringy
like tall spaghetti.

Momma says we can go blind looking in the direction of the sun, so I wear my Daddy's "cool dude" sunglasses...

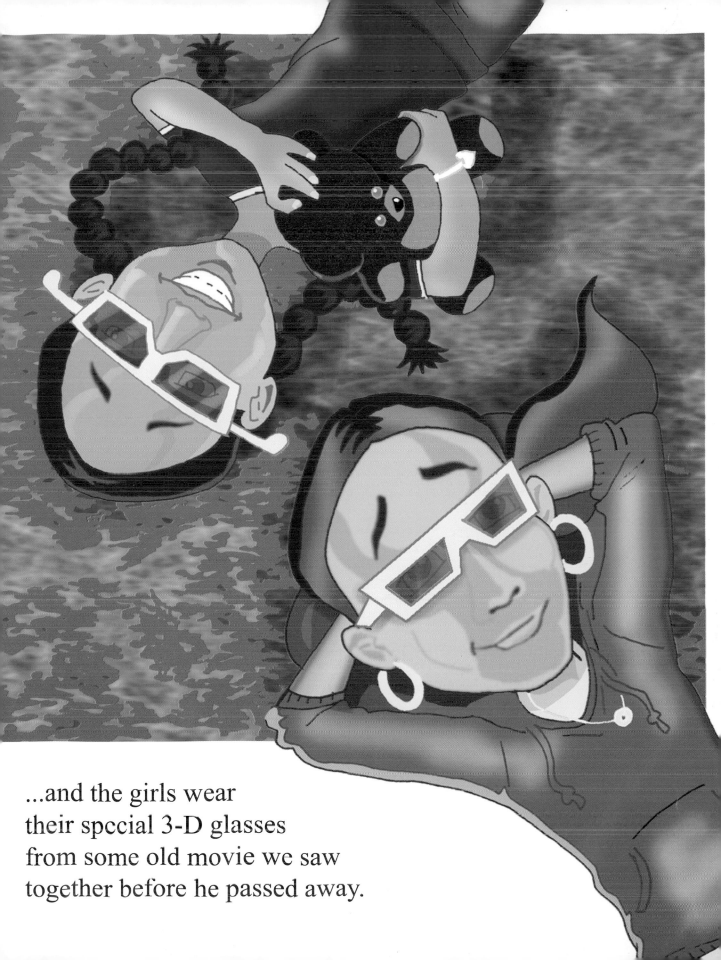

...and the girls wear
their special 3-D glasses
from some old movie we saw
together before he passed away.

Now the trick to cloud watching is to close your eyes really tight, count to five out loud, and then open.

You can see dots of color behind your eyelids, and then when you look at the sky, it's all jiggly with streaks of color and shapes!

I
see a
puppy,
a cat,
and a
choo
choo
train!

You ALWAYS see a train!"
says Camaryn.

I see a horse with wings
on the back of its feet,
and a carrot in its mouth!

What do you see, Cheyenne?

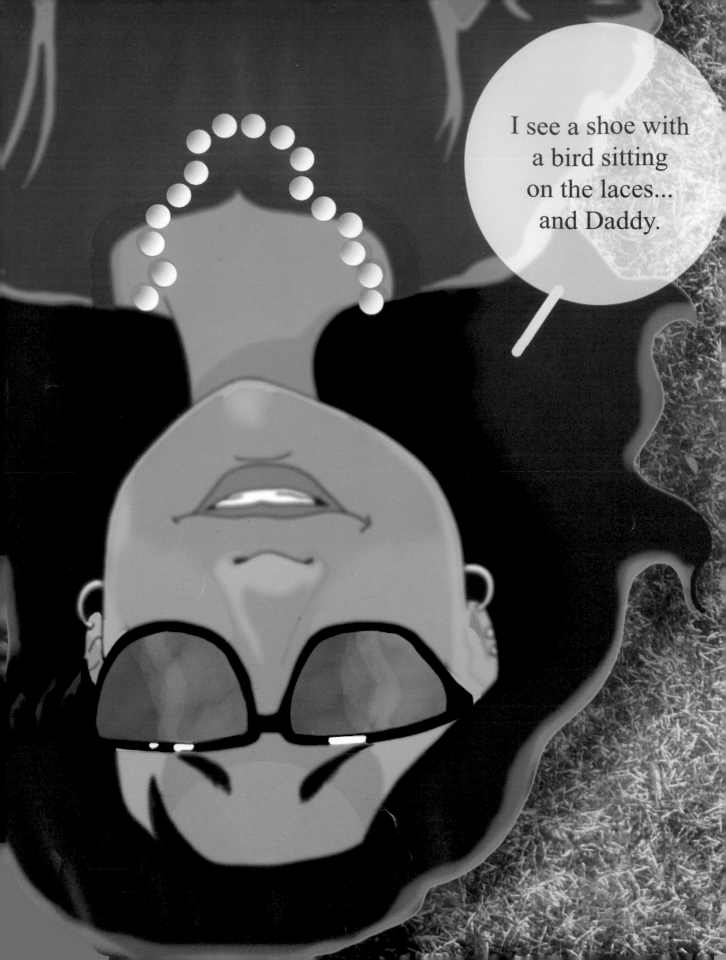

Do you remember when he would tell jokes at the dinner table and we'd laugh so hard we could barely finish our food?

What about when he would cook for Momma?
His "Friday Special" fried-like-a-rock pork
chops and baked-forever chicken?

We didn't like it, it was too hard for us to chew. But Momma LOVED it!

I remember him scooping me up in his strong arms to dance salsa...

....And you two would sit on his feet holding on to the bottom of his legs.

I bet it's a lot easier dancing on a cloud.

Yeah and I bet the pork chops and chicken are softer too!

I know that Daddy loves us very much, and we had a good time together.

We'll never forget the smile on his face or the laughter.

And just when you think you can't remember what he looks like, we can go outside, lay face up to the sky...

...and look for him in a cloud.

The End

THE STORY BEHIND THE STORY

Margo Candelario

MARGO SCOTT was born in San Bernardino, California. She moved to New York at the age of seventeen, where her interest in the arts and culture flourished. Ten years later, she married Phil Candelario. After having their first daughter, the threesome relocated to the state of Georgia seeking a slower pace and healthier environment. Tragically, a few years later, Phil suffered a massive heart attack at the age of thirty-four, leaving three children with questions and fear of death and separation.

Uncomfortable leaving three small children in the care of strangers, Ms. Candelario resurrected her talent for storytelling and writing to create an income while also helping others who have suffered, or are presently suffering, from the loss of a parent. She speaks to youth about her triumph over tragedy and lectures to adults at universities throughout the state of Georgia on the subject of struggle and strength as a single parent.

Phil and Cheyenne

Looking to the Clouds for Daddy is her second collaboration with long-time friend Jerry Craft who also illustrated *Take Me To The Water*, a collection of her poetry that had her nominated *Author of the Year* by the Georgia Writers' Association. She is an accomplished, award-winning visual artist with works exhibited from Hawaii to the eastern seaboard. She currently resides in Georgia with her three daughters.

Camaryn, Trae and Cheyenne

JERRY CRAFT is a New York native and a graduate of the School Of Visual Arts. He is the creator of *Mama's Boyz*, an award-winning comic strip that has been distributed by King Features Syndicate since 1995, making him one of the few syndicated African-American cartoonists in the country.

He has published two books, *Mama's Boyz: As American As Sweet Potato Pie!* and *Mama's Boyz: Home Schoolin'*. His comics have also been featured in the best-selling *Chicken Soup for the African American Soul* and *Chicken Soup for the African American Woman's Soul*.

Jerry Craft

Jerry is the former Editorial Director of the Sports Illustrated For Kids website, and has done illustrations for *Essence Magazine*, comic books, greeting cards, book covers, and his first children's book, *Hillary's Big Business Adventure*. He resides in Connecticut with his wife Autier and his two sons, Jaylen and Aren.

BACK IN THE DAY Margo first met Jerry almost thirty years ago when, at the age of seventeen, she and her mother moved from California to the Washington Heights section of New York City. Jerry welcomed Margo with open arms, and the two have been great friends ever since.

Jerry & Margo (1981)